When You Fall in Love and War

When You Fall in Love and War

Expect the Unexpected

Doubty Noble

INDEX

PROLOGUE

I was sitting in my room on my study chair and when I looked at the picture hanging on the wall it reminded me of all those days when all of us were together. And by us I mean all my friends the members of the youth club which has now taken a different form. I called everyone thereafter and we all- kamal, Jagdeep and Navdeep we all decided to meet at the same place where we all used to sit together for meetings and where all of this begins. It was house which was just few steps away from mine. The owner of the house left it vacant when I was a kid, he went to Canada and thereafter it was only used either for smoking and drinking or later on by our youth club.

We were meeting after 5 years. Kamal who had become a great singer was very busy with his shows and performances still managed to take out time for that meet. Jagdeep and Navdeep went to Canada and settled there for a better life and I was here still struggling and experimenting with my life. All three of them were waiting for me to start the conversation but this time there was nothing serious to be discussed as earlier. Navdeep asked me about Gurleen but I ignored him and started with something else, but in the back of my mind whole scenario of my past flashed and I went into a deep thought. Gurleen was the girl whom I met during my college time.

After a long chit chat we started talking about the house and how it all started. At one point of time in our lives we were at the peak and next moment we were apart from each other. Sometimes you have to look beyond your dreams and plans for your own family, and this is what made us leave everything aside and go for our careers instead of this youth club. It all started when we joined Khalsa College in Amritsar.

FIRST DAY IN COLLEGE

After finishing with my 12th class studies in humanities I decided to continue with the same in the college which was nearest to me, Not only nearest but one of the most famous colleges of Punjab. Since my marks were good in boards so I got admission very easily and that too in humanities.

Many people were disappointed by my decision to choose this subject as it was only taken by those people who wanted to enjoy college life to the fullest and don't want to study any further. But for me it was totally different prospective. I entered the college with a dream to become IPS officer and for that humanities was the best option available for me.

As I entered, I saw a different environment, different from school, different from what I had heard about college life and different from what I had expected. I was welcomed by senior students of my stream. One of them took my bag and asked me to perform something to get my bag back.

I just smiled back at them and they all were quite shocked. "MY friend you are extremely wrong if you think you can make me do anything without my will." After hearing this everyone was furious and angry upon me but I could see some people coming in my support. That was the first time I met Navdeep, Kamal and Jagdeep. In few minutes whole college was there and finally the hustle between seniors and juniors was stopped by the guards out there.

After that I thanked three of them for supporting me. We had formal intro amongst us.

Starting with Navdeep, almost 6ft tall, muscular man with fair complexion and very good dressing sense. He was good at public speaking and was very much interested in local politics; he was admired by most of the girls of the college. He was like Casanova and used to say that, "There is no girl on this planet who crossed my way and hasn't looked back at me." And he was very much correct.

Kamal lived next door to Navdeep. He was very simple guy who always aspired to be the greatest singer of all times. He was totally opposite to Navdeep, very shy in case of girls but while he was within his comfort zone, you can't find better comedian then him.

Next was Jagdeep who was aimless in his life. He was perfect example of the students who join college with humanities just to enjoy and nothing else. He was a person with unlimited cash all the times and had good relations with politicians of the area. He was a person with IQ level at the top but the only thing that was lacking in him was his will of not to do anything great in life.

And finally after having our tea in canteen we all went toward our class. It was LH- 21, a big room with chairs and tables placed in rows and columns in perfection, there were steps going up as we moved back toward the last seats. There were motivational charts and poster on walls of the classroom. In front of class there was a big screen and a white board and some markers of different colours kept beside the big white board. It was very much different from that in our school, but it was quite amazing first lecture of my college life.

First lecture was by Chopra sir; he was our geography teacher and was very strict about discipline in the college. No wonders that he was aware about the hustle which happened in the morning. As he entered the class he inquired about me, but to my surprise he neither scolded me nor talked to me about that incident. He just smiled and started with his lecture. Whole class was listening to him carefully I was sitting on the first bench while other three were back benchers. One after another teachers came in taught us and went back and finally the first day of college was over.

INTER-COLLEGES CUP

After few days, all first year students came to know about college and how it functions and ours was the only batch which could understand that within a time span of less than a month. All because of us, we four were most popular in our batch as we were the only one who saved everyone from ragging. As we were gaining popularity we were unaware that this popularity is not only limited to students. Gradually all the teachers and even principal of our college came to know about us.

Dr. K S Dhillon was college principal, when he was in the campus not even a single student dared to break any rule but for us it was a daily routine to be in front of his office. Every time it was only because of our fights with the senior students, but he always supported us as we were not doing anything wrong. I always believed that if you are not wrong on your part then you need not to worry about anything.

Within few months we were followed by all the students in the college and this time even seniors were along with us. Everyone supported us because we were working for a good cause and in addition to that we four together made a deadly combination which people used to say- Kanwar's mind, Navdeep's strength, Kamal's voice and Jagdeep's money. No one was there in the college who could beat us in any of these things.

By the mid of the second semester we were heading towards the inter colleges cup, which was held in every three years and this time it was going to be hosted by our college. Any competition which a person can imagine was there in that cup. I got selected in volleyball team while Navdeep and Jagdeep were there in the football team and as expected Kamal was selected for the singing competition.

Though it was very tough selection procedure but we all managed to be there in the mains rather than being in the cheering party or for that matter in the reserves. It was quite surprising for seniors to see that we were again there in their events and they were made to stand outside. Whole college had high expectations from all of us as such the competition was in our own college.

Now our college timings were rescheduled. We were only made to do practise and nothing else. We were allowed to bunk as many lectures as we want and we were provided with some extra perks and privileges. After our practices we four used to sit together at one place, which was generally canteen or in any one of our houses.

Our bond of friendship was admired by our all students in the college and even our parents liked that too much. When anyone of us was missing in any photograph of ours, people used to ask other three that why is the fourth one with you.

After a long waited time it was finally the time for inter-colleges cup. Our main competitor was DAV College for boys. Day one, basketball and athletics were held along with painting competition. We were able to perform well in athletics but we came third in basketball. However in painting competition we were ahead of DAV.

Day two it was time for hockey, handball and dance competition. Unfortunately we lost in hockey and handball to DAV, but dance was our strong point. It is said that if you want to see real folk dance of Punjab you must meet the dance club of Khalsa College. Day 3 was the final day and before that the scores were

Khalsa College-26
DAV College- 28
GNDU-19
LPU-16
Chandigarh University-17
Punjab University-20

Last day of the cup and we were still two points behind from DAV College. The events which were left were Volleyball, Football and Singing competition. The only way to win the cup was to win in all three competitions left. First event was singing and without even giving a second thought to it kamal was declared as winner however DAV College came second in that. It was a tough fight going on. Then it was my event finals of the volleyball match against DAV. We were losing in that match the set difference was 2-0 and had been the next set gone to them we were done there.

All hopes of winning the cup would have been gone. But then our team captain came with a new plan of combination attack which we had never practised earlier. It was a great gamble but the luck favoured us that day and we won the next two sets. Now the set score was 2-2 and finally the deciding set was there. After lot of efforts we won that set too which made us settle the score with DAV. Now it was 28 all.

Final event was football and in that too the final was with DAV College. Football was always a strong point of our college and because of Navdeep and Jagdeep in the team we were pretty sure that we were going to win the match and the cup too. But to our bad luck Navdeep got injured in the starting minutes of the match. The whole team was low on josh thereafter. But somehow our team managed to play draw against them and now it was time for penalty shootouts.

First penalty they scored but we didn't. Same thing happened for the second time and now the score was 2-0. Last chance if we score we survive, if not we lose the match and cup too. And there came Jagdeep for taking the penalty and he scored.

Our keeper saved the goal too. Now it was 2-1 but still we were one goal behind. Fourth penalty was taken by the senior most player of our team, and here we go we scored again and they missed it. Now the score was 2-2.

6 Now it was last chance for both the teams. Oh no we missed that last penalty. Ball just hit the pole and came out. All of us were sad for it is too difficult for a goalkeeper to save a goal in that condition but fortune favours the brave and finally he stopped the last penalty.

This was most exciting moment in the history of inter colleges cup. Sudden death in football match which could make the difference in the cup winner. First was DAV's turn and they missed the shot. Navdeep in spite of being injured decided that he will take that penalty. Team captain and Whole College was shocked by his decision but I was sure that he will score. And he didn't prove me wrong, he scored. We won the match and the cup too.

NEW YEAR NEW THINGS

First year in college went very smooth. As we all sailed towards the second year we could not see the high tide in the sea. I got 'A' grade in all subjects while Kamal got B+ and other two got B grade, but these grades didn't matter because we all were heading toward something different in our lives.

Navdeep met a girl in the college. Komal, she was one of the most beautiful girls in the college. She was crush of almost half of the college boys but taken by none except for the man who she thought deserved her. I don't know how Navdeep managed but within one month of their first meeting their relationship status changed from single to committed.

But we three were very happy for him as he got the hottest chick by his side. I used to say to other two that it's all about wasting your time. They too thought the same way but Navdeep being a stud considered it essential for him to have a girl friend during the college time. This made him a little bit away from our group but it didn't affect us much. We still managed to be together on weekends and celebrate life.

Kamal used to have extra classes for his singing practise so he got busy with that and Jagdeep was planning his tour abroad to Australia just for fun. And finally I was left alone who had nothing to do but to study for IPS. But someone told me that it's too early to start as such I was having two complete years to go for my exam. So I used to roam around here and there in my village and play with the people around.

One day while I was walking on the way to my house I found my neighbour, Sumit lying on the path. I got scared at first but then I realised my responsibility to take him to hospital. I went running towards my house got my car and took him to the hospital. In the meanwhile people around informed his parents and they arrived there with a tensed face. I called my friend for if any money was required in emergency.

We were standing outside the ICU and waiting for the doctor. When he came outside he said something which Sumit's parents could not believe. He was addicted to drugs and got overdosed by drugs. For a time being I was also shocked by what doctor said. I knew Sumit from a long time and I had never seen him doing anything wrong. He could not be a drug addict, I couldn't believe my ears that 18 years old boy is a drug addict but it was sad truth.

After 24hrs doctors were able to recover him from the heart attack but he was not in his senses.

Many days passed I was waiting for him to come home and finally when he was brought back I didn't waste a minute and went to his house. I asked him the reason behind the drugs consumption. He didn't reply to me at that time, may be his mother was near that's why. I always treated him as younger brother and I could not believe that my brother could ever behave like he did. I asked his mother to bring something to eat for him and she went towards the kitchen.

When we were alone in his room I asked him again the same question. Tears came rolling down his eyes as he replied, "Bhayia, it all started few months back when you told me to go out and start playing with the boys outside. I went there, for few days I was not allowed to play when I asked the reason they said you need to prove that you can do anything for the sake of game. I asked them what should I do and they gave me this white powder and told me to sniff it in one go. I was not aware what it was but after doing that I feel different level of energy in my body and then I started playing. I felt the need of that powder next day for playing and again they gave it to me. This is how I

got addicted to it bhayia please save me, it is killing me from inside bhayia please." He started crying at him maximum voice. I tried to stop him from doing that and consoled him.

IDEA OF YOUTH CLUB

I was not able to sleep that day. I called three of them in a conference and talked to them about the matter. They were also disturbed after listening to the whole story. "We must do something for this. I don't know how many people are affected by this drug addiction but we must try to save their lives." I said with a firm voice.

Kamal replied, "Kanwar it is very difficult to bring a person back to his normal life that has been addicted to drugs. And even if we start doing that we will in the wrong side for all those who are selling these drugs." Navdeep and Jagdeep were having similar thoughts.

I said in very emotional tone, "Yes you are right we can't do anything about this, all we can do is that have parties and celebrate our fake victories, all we can do is that we can curse the system while chit chatting in a group and all we can do is that we can say that we are the best and we can do everything but the reality is when it comes to real job we all take step back. Everyone in Punjab want that Bhagat Singh should take birth again but nobody wants him to take birth at his house. Every day we hear lot of cases of drug abuse but we ignore them just because of a simple reason that it is not happening with us. But is it right to do that? Someone has to take initiative against this then why not us?"

For few seconds it was complete silence then in low voice Jagdeep asked, "So what are your plans?" I had nothing to say at that time so I asked them to give me some time to think over it. They all agreed to it. For many days, I was thinking about Sumit only, I was not able to focus on my studies and dedicated all my time towards this problem of drug abuse.

"Youth Club?" Navdeep asked in a vague manner. "Yes my friend youth club. We will ask for volunteers for this project through this club. Initially we will tell people that it is just a club to motivate people to play various games and to stay fit in life. As you all know that how crazy people are, when it comes to their fitness. But our main focus will be on stopping this addiction of drugs from people's mind." I replied.

Everyone in the group agreed to this idea and was ready take down this challenge. Now the first task was to decide the place to do all these things. Obviously it was something not to be done in college campus so we decided not to involve college area in this.

I don't know how but suddenly an idea strike in my mind, "Why don't we use the place where all of this began?" When I asked Sumit about the place where he used to do all this he told me about the house which was vacant since we were kids. I decided to make that as our work place. That would be our first victory over drugs.

Nobody used drugs in open and nobody was ready to sell or purchase in the light of the day. All these things were done during the darkest hours of the night. But we were about to occupy the place where all this business of drugs was done.

I asked my dad to give call to the owner of that house and tell him that we need that house for our club. I didn't tell my parents the whole reason behind this. They were only aware about the fitness and all but not about the war which we were going to start against the drugs.

We got the house and we were all set to begin with our club. We accomplished our first aim when we made that house a good place to live. It was no more used for smoking or drinking or for that matter consuming drugs. Our next aim was to motivate people to play various games and to stay fit.

"A strong does whatever he wants and weak suffers whatever he must." This was the tag line of our club and was one of the main sources of attraction for people. With help of Jagdeep's father we were able to purchase all the gym equipment within few months.

By the end of third semester we were able to make that house a perfect health club which provides various supplements and nutrition items for those people who wanted to stay fit. We also talked to our college principal about this and he motivated us and said, "Tell me if you need anything from my side or from college. I will make sure that you will not face any problem regarding your lecture shortage but you will have to pass on your own." After that we were officially allowed to bunk the lectures.

NEW CHAPTER OF MY LIFE

Our club was gaining popularity and finally it was registered as an official NGO in the block. Because of the club we were not able to attend classes sometimes and sometimes we bunked for the whole day. Our seniors took advantage of the situation and again the ragging thing started in our college. We placed a suggestion box outside that house and one day I found a chit in that.

I took the chit out and it read, "Sir I know you are working for a good cause here but few people have started talking advantage of your absence from the college. Ragging by senior students of our college has started again. Since you are not there, no one is taking initiative to stop them. Please come to college and help us."

I went into a deep thought that why people are so afraid of stopping the wrong things. They need to know when to say no, they must become strong otherwise the stronger will do whatever he want and weak will as such suffer whatever he must. I decided to go to college without three Navdeep Kamal and Jagdeep so that by seeing us together seniors may not get alert. I was there in stealth mode hiding behind the public when I saw a group of people disturbing every girl that was passing by. I send message to my friends to reach college as soon as possible.

I straight away went to them and got engaged in a fight. At first it was just verbal but then they said something about my family in front of the whole college. I didn't bother to wait for my friends and slapped one of them. "Oh no Kanwar Singh you are alone and they have heavily outnumbered you. But now you have only two options fight or flight. Second option seems perfect but you are man enough to handle them by your own."

While I was thinking, whole college came in my support. Now we had heavily outnumbered them. They flee from the place of incident and I was cheered by whole college. Before my friend came it was all done. They were very angry on me for I didn't tell them anything. But it was alright now the matter was solved and finally students were happy.

Next day, there was again one letter in that suggestion box and this it was addressed to me only. Who could that be? I thought and started reading it, "Sir, I am the girl whom you saved yesterday from seniors. I was about to leave the college but your actions yesterday prevented me from doing that. I would like to thank you for that. I had heard from many people in the college that you always help others and you are working for a good cause. I also want to join your club with your permission. Can we meet tomorrow in canteen at 12?"

"What? A girl wants to join our club and wants to meet me for that." I started wondering how it was possible. I decided to go and meet her. Again I kept this little secret along with me and went to college next day without three of them. I went to canteen by 11:45 and sat there on a table for two. "Okay, only 15 minutes are there. Let me wait for her." I gave it a thought and finally dot 12 o clock a girl came near me and said hello.

Oh wow........

She was god damn beautiful. She was wearing red suit which was looking perfect with her extremely fair complexion. Black hairs and brown eyes and her face cuts made a deep impression on my heart. Black mole on her cheek was another addition to her face which made me fall for her even more. She was the most beautiful girl whom I had ever seen in my entire life.

Before I could say anything she began, "Thank you sir for saving me that day. I just wanted to thank you in personal. My dad is DSP and if I would have told him anything he would have taken severe action against college and I didn't want anything of that sort happening in my college. The courage which you showed that day was extra-ordinary...."

I smiled and started in between, "I was just doing what I felt right at that time and I always used to say that if you are not wrong you need not to worry about anything. And first of all stop calling me sir. You can call me by my name. By the way what's your name? Let's begin with your intro"

"Now you are trying to do ragging with me, isn't it", she said smiling and continued, "My name is Gurleen and I belong to Amritsar only. I have opted for BSc. Biology after completing my 12th from Khalsa college public school. I am very much interested to join your club." After that she started smiling.

"Want to have something?" I almost forgot about that but finally I asked after half of our conversation was over. I ordered coffee for both of us and it was served in next 5 minutes till then we were quite waiting for the coffee to come as if it will break the awkward silence.

With the first sip of my coffee I asked, "So why do you want to join our club? It has been almost three months that our club has started and till now not even a single girl has opted for it." She was quite for some time and after that she said, "I got two reasons for that, the first one is that I love being fit in life and the second one is I know what are your actual plans."

I give it a thought and said, "OK I will talk to other three heads of the club and will let you know." We exchanged our mobile numbers and that was the end of our first meeting over a cup of coffee.

THE SUDDEN CHANGE

After that meet, I started going to college almost every day just to meet Gurleen, while the other three members of the club were focusing on the youth club. One day Navdeep asked me to tell them the reason behind my regularity in college.

It was time to tell them the truth and ask them about the addition of a new active member in the club. They were surprised when I told them the whole story. Jagdeep started cursing himself that why he left the letter in the suggestion box for me to read it.

It's all about being lucky and at that time my good luck was at the peak. Later on I was able to convince everyone that it will not affect our club any more but she will be a plus point for our club as she was the daughter of deputy superintendent of police of the area. All of them agreed to the point of adding her to the club.

I gave a call to Gurleen to inform her as soon as they all gave a yes call. Kamal said in very notorious tone, "Ha ha go call her, now she is going to take priority over us." Navdeep replied laughing, "Leave it yaar; he is not in his senses. He has completely fallen for her. By the way does she know that you like her and what are her views about you?"

After saying good bye to Gurleen I came back to them. They were making fun out me because I used to say that, this is just waste of time and nothing else. But when you start feeling something for someone special then you don't care about your time being wasted. Navdeep again asked me whether she liked me the same way that I did. I had no reply for that because even I was not aware about how she felt about me at that time.

After few days I asked Gurleen to visit our club house and when she came, she was amazed by the way we had managed things so far. By then she was ready to be the part of it. We were total 49 members working for the club at that time and with the addition of Gurleen the count reached 50.

At that time we were proud of ourselves for we were growing at very fast rate. I was looking after the choreography team of the club who would be going to different villages and were to perform various acts relating to fitness and drug abuse. Gurleen also joined the same part of the club.

Now it was not only college but in the club too we were together. Now she was completely frank with me. She didn't hesitate while talking to me. We used to talk about our families, friends, hobbies, our dreams and what not. The road of love on which I started travelling was not going to end but I was still not aware that whether she felt the same way or not.

I didn't have any idea to confirm that but I was OK with that. After she came to the club I felt a sudden change in the working of the club house. She had such a beautiful nature that she made the club house alive. I could see everyone working with great enthusiasm and we all were very happy with that.

One day Navdeep told me, "At first I thought that she will create problem for our club but I was wrong. We must take a chance at women empowerment and should allow other girls also to be a part of it." When we told this to Kamal and Jagdeep they both agreed and we started working upon it. We asked our batch mates and told Gurleen to popularise the club amongst her batch mates.

The plan worked and it was a great success. Within a month the total strength of our club crossed 150. The reason being when girls started joining the club, all the boys who had crush on them were willing to join. For that we made a terms and condition form on which sincerity towards the club matter was written in bold letters.

We divided the club into three teams after that. First one was the fitness team which was headed by Navdeep, second was the choreography team for which I was made in charge and the third one was games team which was handled by

Jagdeep. Kamal was made president of the club and he was responsible for planning each and every activity of the club.

SOMETHING DIFFERENT

Last few months of the second year brought many challenges in our lives. We were able to create a spark in the teenager to focus more on their fitness rather than drugs, I was on the verge to propose Gurleen and we decided to take part in the college elections for our final year. In between these entire things we were completely unaware about the fact that we were getting on the nerves of drug dealers.

It was the month April, the month in which farmers are the happiest people of the world, the month in which crops are about to be harvested. The efforts and hard work of the farmer from ploughing the land to sowing the seed, from watering his crops to protecting them from weed all are shown as a result by his crops. And the same was with our club. The land was right and the seed was sown. We gave water as per requirement but we were not able to protect it from weed.

This weed was the drug dealers who could not bear their business going down. Their main head was Baljeet. He started threatening the main members of the club however they were not able to do anything to four of us but, Gurleen was not able to handle that pressure.

When we were four, people used to say that nobody can beat us but with the addition of one new member the whole situation changed. As soon as Gurleen started getting warnings like that she informed her dad. Her dad told her to leave the club with immediate effect but she was not ready to.

Her dad explained her, "listen Gurleen, I am your dad and I always cared for your dreams but right now your safety is my priority. You don't have any idea about how far these people can go because when a drug addict doesn't get his dose he is ready to do anything just for the sake of getting a little bit of that. Drugs don't allow a person to think and he only follows the one who can fulfil his need. I will not allow you to be a part of this club anymore and that's all. End of conversation."

For next few days Gurleen didn't come to the club house, I thought that she might be busy with her studies but I was worried when she didn't pick my phone call. I was thinking of proposing her and prepared everything in the college. I set the whole scenario, "Jagdeep, when you see her entering the gate inform me by a message, Navdeep and Komal, you will bring her to LH-15 which remains empty during the morning hours of the college and I will standing beside the door and as she will enter Kamal will pop the balloon which will be having flower petals in that." I also told my club members to prepare some good proposal posters and to paste them on the walls of the LH.

Everything was done and I was fully prepared to propose her with a bouquet of white and red roses. Lecture hall was all set it was full with amazing fragrance and there were posters of I LOVE YOU, YOU ARE THE BEST THING EVER HAPPENED TO ME and many more.

As Gurleen entered the college I got a message from Jagdeep, Navdeep and Komal were bringing her towards the LH-15. With every single step, my heartbeat was increasing. In between Gurleen asked both of them to tell her something about what is going on, but they both smiled and told her to just wait and watch. As soon as she entered the LH, kamal popped the balloon over her head and she was under the shower of petals of red roses.

I finally came in front of her and with one knee on the ground I proposed her, "Gurleen, I have been trying so hard to say you this but I couldn't gather this much courage to do so. But today I want you to feel special because you really are, especially for me. I love the way you talk, I love the way you walk, I love the way you eat, I love the way we meet, I love the way you smile and I love the way you breathe sorry to break the flow of poem and that's all. I love you Gurleen."

After hearing this and seeing all the arrangements which I had done she got emotional. Her eyes were filled with water and she was almost crying. I wanted to wipe her tears but before that I was waiting for her response. She didn't speak anything which made me feel tensed, I was left blank there. "Have I done something wrong? Please reply Gurleen, please say you love me."

I was thinking in my mind and finally she replied, "I had waited for this moment since the day I met you. But I thought that I don't deserve you. I also tried many times to tell you the same thing but then stopped just because I thought you are perfect in every aspect and there was no way that you would accept my proposal. Thank you Kanwar for giving me such a nice surprise. I love you so much."

I couldn't believe myself at that time. I wanted someone to pinch and make me realise that it was not a dream. She accepted the bouquet happily and thereafter we were all set to celebrate that moment. All the club members from the college were there and they had already brought the cake as if they were aware that Gurleen was going to say yes.

It might be true also because usually it happens that when a boy and girl like each other, all the people around are aware of this fact except from both of them. But by then it doesn't matter, we were together thereafter and we promised to be with each other at all the point of time.

Later that week, I threw a party to all the club members to celebrate our love. It was something different in the club house that day; I was feeling very special that day and wanted my Gurleen to feel even more special. When everyone was there I took the opportunity to speak something for love.

With mike in my hand I begin, "Ladies and gentlemen, may I have your attention please, today I would like to say something. Something about love, something about the one whom we all care for and something about the everlasting bond of friendship. You know what, love is very special feeling which I realised since the day I met Gurleen. Before that I used to tell people that it is just a waste of time and let me tell you my views about love are still the same it is a waste of time but now I realise that this waste of time is very important part of our lives."

Gurleen was standing next to me. She hugged me tightly and in few seconds we were kissing each other. People around there started cheering for both of us in a notorious tone. Later on it became an embarrassing moment for us. But we both were happy and were ready to be each other's forever.

After that night we were closer to each other. We decided to tell our parents about our relation because we were about to enter the final year of the college and were ready for our relationship to move one step ahead. Before that also, we used to go to each other's house but our parents thought that we were just good friends and nothing else.

When we told them the truth, we didn't expect that it would change everything. But in love and war it is always said, "Expect the unexpected as everything is fair in love and war." It was not only love but the war was also going on against the drug dealers.

UPS AND DOWNS

I used to share almost everything with my mom before my dad and when I told her she was very happy for me. She had met Gurleen many times as she used to come to our house after the club hours. She told me only one thing, "Beta, first complete your studies and get a good job so that you can be self sufficient to earn for both of you. After that I would be the luckiest mother in law to have a daughter like her."

I was very happy after listening to that. Mom promised me that she would talk to dad and convince him once I will get a good job. It was very simple for me to do that. I would have easily got a job which would have paid me enough to earn for both of us but I choose to become IPS officer by which I would have not only earn money but respect too.

From my side it was all good all set but when Gurleen talked to her father he had a different response, "Is he the same guy who is leading that youth club? So that is the reason you don't want to leave the club. Gurleen try to understand his future is not secure at all. The path on which he is travelling has no u turn and it ends with death. Plus he is not going to get good job because of his fights and aggressive nature. What if he doesn't get a job to fulfil your needs? What if he gets killed while working for his club? What if you and your family get troubled because of him?"

"But dad I love him. You can't do this to your daughter!" Gurleen said in a low and emotional tone.

"No Gurleen, I can't even imagine you in such situation and I will not allow you to marry him at all. And if you don't stop working for that club I will not allow you to go to college. This is my last warning to you and don't worry I will take special care of him when he will visit any police station."

"Can you please give him one chance just because of me?"

After thinking for a while her dad replied, "Listen Gurleen I have no problem with him but his way of living is out of this world. If you can change that then only I can think of something."

In the evening I tried calling her, she didn't answer my call. I text her reading that if something is wrong. I didn't get a reply. Next morning when she came to college her eyes were swollen as if she didn't sleep whole night or cried a lot.

I got little hint about yesterday's conversation with her dad from her eyes. But still I wanted to enquire from her and I went close to her she hugged me tight and started crying. I asked her to calm down and tell what has happened.

She said in fumbling voice, "Kanwar tell me one thing clearly, do you really love me or not?" I was surprised after listening to her and replied, "I proposed you, whole day I stay with you, when you are not present I start feeling incomplete, before going off to sleep and after waking up I talk to you and you still have doubts that I love you or not."

After wiping her tears, I started again.

"I do love you and it can't be measured by anything except by the true love feelings and when it come to true love feeling there is no need of measurement at all. I love you Gurleen and will love you till my last breathe."

Tears from her eyes were not stopping at all. She was crying out loudly in front of the whole college. I took her along with me to an empty LH and asked her about the conversation between her and her parents.

She said something which left me completely blank, "Kanwar listen here if you want to be with me for rest of your life then you need to quit all your club activities." She took a pause and after next thing which she said was next to impossible for me.

"You will have to get a good job and most important is that you need to cut off from your friends. My dad will save you from all the drug dealers and mafias who are behind you only if you stop doing all these things but he can't save you all. Now you have only two options left either you choose me and we will enjoy rest of our life together or you leave me and walk on this death road along with your friends."

ME OR THEM

It is rightly said, "United we rise and divided we fall." And when you strongest point becomes your weakness then there is no chance of your survival, neither in love nor in war.

I was standing on the road which suddenly got split into two. On one side my friends were there willing to die for the cause which I gave them and on one side my love was there willing to live a happy married life.

Gurleen gave me two days time to think and reply to her. It was the most difficult situation in my life. All the things flashed in my mind no one can beat you when you four are together and you are the best couple in the world.

Next two days I didn't meet anyone. I wanted sometime alone to think over again and again. When my mom saw me in that condition she asked me the reason, I didn't say anything. She was worried and she told dad about my condition. She never saw me sad throughout my life and that was the reason for her worries.

When dad came in my room to talk to me I said, "Dad, we have never talked on any serious matter before this but today I really need your help. I want you to answer my question. When you have to choose between your friend and your love what will you choose?"

After hearing that my dad started smiling and replied, "Listen son, you are not the first person who has to choose between the two. Everyone face such condition in his life where he has to choose one option out of the two. Even though it is very difficult to live without both but I will just say that nobody will care for you better than your love and nobody will stand with you better than your friends. Final decision will always be yours but I will say that you must follow your heart."

Men will be men, I got to know that day instead of helping me my dad put me in more confusion. Your love and your friends both are important in your life. Finally I made a firm decision and I was ready to tell Gurleen and my friends. Next day I called Gurleen, Navdeep, Jagdeep and Kamal to LH-15 from where it all started as such Gurleen was not ready to go to club house.

All of them came and when Gurleen asked me to tell my answer I began, "Gurleen you have put me in this grave situation. The decision which I am going to take today is going to affect many lives. It was not easy for me to decide, when it comes to a war between love and friendship you can't afford to lose any one of them but sometime life has different plans for you. Sometimes it gives you so much that you are not able to handle it and sometimes it takes everything in just a blink of an eye. Today I am going to lose one half of me. And finally I choose my friends over my love."

Everyone in that LH was shocked. It was very emotional moment everyone's eyes were filled with tears for some it were tears of happiness and for some it were tears of sadness.

Gurleen didn't say anything to me. She smiled at me and went outside. I could see that she went crying. She went outside the college. I ran behind her and tried to stop her to explain my reason but she was not ready to listen. She drove her car and went away as I was moving toward the road. I tried to call her, texted her many times but she was not ready to talk to me.

HOSPITAL

I went back to my friends and tried to console me for my loss. Kamal in order to make me feel good tried out his best jokes but that could not make me get over the loss. After half an hour I got a call from Gurleen. I was very happy that at least she is ready to talk to me but it was not her. Someone picked her phone and called me to inform that Gurleen met with an accident and was being taken to the Arora hospital.

We all rushed to Arora hospital. After inquiring from the reception we came to know that she was in EMERGENCY Operation Theatre. Doctors told that she was not stable. Next 48 hours were very critical. I called Gurleen's dad to inform him and he was shocked after hearing this. In next half an hour he reached hospital.

He told me to stay away from Gurleen, which was next to impossible for me. I tried to explain him that we both love each other and can't live without each other. He warned me that if I or for that matter any of my friend seen near the hospital would be facing severe consequences. He thought that we would be deeply affected by his warning but nobody was there to stop us. At that point to time I considered it right to leave the hospital and let DSP Sidhu stay there for her daughter.

After two days I went to the hospital before going for college to pay a visit to Gurleen. Her dad couldn't control his anger after seeing me and called his men to come to hospital. I was aware of what was coming next but stood still there trying to convince her dad and this time I didn't even call my friends for back up. After few minutes I could see few police men coming toward me. They took me along with them and outside the hospital they started beating me. I was brutally attacked with sticks and shoes and lost my conscious after few hits.

Since our college was near to the hospital so somehow Jagdeep got a call from a student of our college regarding my situation. In no time almost half of the college was there. Jagdeep called his dad and told him everything. Also police men were aware of Jagdeep's political link so they left me there only and went away on their bikes.

I was lying almost dead there and very soon I was lying on the hospital bed in the room next to Gurleen. The pain of my body was nothing in front of the pain that I was feeling in my heart. Gurleen met with accident just because of me, my whole group was now in trouble because of me. I had nothing to do but to curse myself for all the things I had done.

After 3 days I was discharged from the hospital but Gurleen was still there. She had several head injuries because of which she was still in ICU. I could not stop thinking about her. I just wanted to be with her but the decision which I took for my friends was taking me away from her. She loved me so much, she wanted my secure future but I thought about my dreams over her. At one point of time she made my dreams her but I could not do the same for her.

But you only know you love her when you let her go. This song stroked in my mind every day and night. For few days I was not able to concentrate on the club activities. Navdeep told me to take rest for few days and after that begin with a fresh start. I agreed to him. While I was at home I tried to call Gurleen but she didn't pick my calls. I texted her long SMS to apologise but I couldn't find any single message of her in my inbox.

END OF LOVE

It was the last month of the second year when we all started working on the club again. There was a conference for the NGOs in Delhi. We decided to go there so that more and more people would know about our club and then we would be on the national platform instead of working only in Punjab.

Our stay in Delhi was getting very boring, one day Navdeep told, "Guys, I have plan for today. Let's go to an uninvited party and enjoy there. I have heard that parties in Delhi are too much fun."

At first it seems senseless to do that but then we all agreed to that because as such we were free with nothing to do but to somehow kill time. So we all dressed up, suited-booted went to Hyatt Regency hotel.

It seemed like that the party was organised by highly reputed person as many political leaders were present there. To our luck Jagdeep's uncle was also present there. Jagdeep went to him and told him that we were uninvited guest in the party. He told him not to worry and enjoy the party.

As we were roaming around the place, I saw Gurleen there, my heart skipped a beat. I told Navdeep, Kamal and Jagdeep about her presence in the party. By the time they could find her she just disappeared.

"Are you drunk? How many drinks have you gulped in till now?" Kamal questioned because no one amongst them could see Gurleen.

"No buddy seriously, I have seen her and this time I am not assuming that. I saw her in this party and look her dad is also here." After seeing her dad I said.

"Now all we need is to stay away from her dad and find her if she exist in this party." Jagdeep said after we started moving away from DSP Sidhu. As we were walking away I saw Gurleen standing alone at one corner of the party hall.

I went to her and said hi, she was surprised seeing me there at the party. She acted normally, the excitement which I was expecting was not there. Not being aware of the reason I straight away said, "I love you so much Gurleen. Let's be together again. I miss you so much. I badly need you back in my life. Please I request you to come back."

"Kanwar if you would have told me this thing at that time. We would have been together forever. But now it's too late I can't help it." Gurleen said replying in a sad tone.

"What has happened Gurleen? We used to live for each other and now it's too difficult for me to live without you. It is same as breathing for me. Please don't do this to me. I can't live without you."

"You don't know what I have gone through in these past few months. But you didn't care at that time you didn't even considered visiting me once at the hospital. I was waiting for you but you didn't come and now when I have everything in my life you want to come back and ruin everything." Gurleen said in a firm voice uplifting her above tears.

"What do you mean by everything? We were each other's everything."

She was still normal and replied, "What are you talking about? We were never together and we never will be. We were just good friends and nothing more. It was all a blunder which happened to me just because your repo was good in college. I was attracted to you only because of this."

"Please don't say this." My heart was broken.

"Now I have a boyfriend who makes me a priority over his friends and for that matter his work. He is not like you. Oh sorry for my words you are not like him, rather you are nothing in front of him."

I broke into tears in the mid of the conversation which I thought was over from my side. Navdeep was silently observing us from a distance. After seeing me in that condition he rushed toward us.

"Oh so all of you are here. Who invited you in this party? Should I call my dad right now?"

"What happened Gurleen why is he crying? I thought after meeting you he would be the happiest person here but I am seeing totally opposite of that." Navdeep questioned her.

In the mean while one guy came and stood near her. "What happened Gurleen? Who are these guys? Never met them before!" He exclaimed.

"Oh they are my college friends and let me take this opportunity to introduce you to all of them. Meet my fiancé."

Navdeep burst out in anger and started abusing both of them. He was loud enough to catch everyone's attention. Jagdeep and Kamal also came near us. Now we were the centre of attraction of the party. Everyone was looking at us and then Gurleen started speaking.

"That's enough don't utter even a single word from your mouth. All of you know what your friend did to me and now you want that I should forget all this. How could you even think that?"

Before she could speak anything further her fiancé punched Navdeep on his face. That was it. Now it was difficult to control Navdeep but I came between in his way and stopped him.

"Leave it Navdeep we should not fight for the thing which don't belong to us." I said and we left from there. I straight away went to my car and started crying out loud. All three of them tried to console me but it was hard for me. I was very depressed after that and decided not to attend the conference. Navdeep and Jagdeep went for the conference while Kamal was trying to handle me and control me while I was drunk and crying in the hotel room.

In this way the second year ended and took the most precious person in my life away from me. I tried many ways to forget her somehow but I failed in doing that. Now it was only my friends and the youth club who were standing against drugs and the people dealing with them.

COLLEGE ELECTIONS

Third year began with a bang as we were heading toward the new challenge which was just one month away i.e. college elections. It was one of the major events of Amritsar as it decided the majority of youth towards a political party. We decided to make a new party rather than joining any other existing party. We named it Youth Club Student Union (Y.C.S.U). Kamal was chosen as the face for our election. He was going for the president seat in the college while we all others were supporting him. Being the president of college give you control of the whole college and the best part was that college students could be utilised for our club activities.

Khalsa College was perfect in every aspect of administration at that time. There was no other agenda for our elections, so we choose anti ragging and fitness. It was very easy for us to do that in fact we were doing that without any support or help. Our rival was none other than Harpreet who was supported by few students who lived on drugs and obviously his uncle Baljeet. He was having money and that's all. Not many students were ready to support him but he was ready to buy student's votes with his uncle's money.

Jagdeep was ready to spend money for elections but I told him that we will not use any unfair means to win this elections. MP of Amritsar was in our support because of Jagdeep and also because of the lok sabha elections. We requested him that we don't want any external interference in college election and we wanted to win them on our own. He promised us that he will not interfere until and unless someone other try to do so.

Campaigning for elections were going on with full enthusiasm. We used to say, "Our victory is sure only announcement is left." Until one tragedy took place. After seeing our reputation Harpreet decided to get the elections postponed or for that matter cancelled. He planned something which we couldn't even think of. Two days were left for the college elections. Students had already decided their next president but Harpreet succeeded in his plan. That evening we four were taking a round of the college premises when Kamal told us that he wanted to go for his music practise. After saying that he went back to the parking lot. Within next one minute I got a call saying that Harpreet has planned to shoot Kamal.

I was getting this feeling of something wrong but didn't say anything. We rushed toward the parking lot toward which Kamal was heading. I called him but he didn't pick my call. Finally we saw him and shouted for him to stop. He was safe; we went near him and started laughing in joy. We were not able to control breathe. When he listened to our reason of stopping him he also started laughing and said that someone might had played prank.

We all started thinking that way but it was not a prank. Jagdeep saw two people on bike coming towards us. He suspected pistol in ones' hand. The man with pistol was about shoot Kamal when Jagdeep came in between and bullet pierced through his right shoulder. We were all shocked at that moment. After firing a shot those people on bike disappeared from that area. We were near the parking lot. Navdeep rushed toward his car and brought it near Jagdeep. He drove as fast as he could to the hospital.

Jagdeep was out of danger because the bullet hit him in the shoulder. But how did they enter the campus area was the question striking in my mind, as such they were not college students. Finally the matter was gone to principal and he called Kamal and Harpreet and asked them if he should postpone the elections or not. We also went along with him.

We opposed it to a great extend as such we were winning but Harpreet and his party was ready for elections to be postponed. This discussion turned into debate and then gradually into fight in the principal's office. Everything went wrong and we all were suspended for two weeks. Till that time the elections were postponed and we were given warning that if we enter the college area our ticket for election would be cancelled.

On one side Jagdeep was lying on hospital bed and on other side we all were suspended. I was feeling quite low at that time and the thought that if Gurleen would have been here the situation would have been different. This made me feel even low and I was completely down. The main thing striking in my at that time was that who were those guys on bike and how did they entered the college. I was having only two weeks to figure it out.

CULPRIT BEHIND THE SCENE

From next day I started the enquiry on my own while Kamal was looking after elections and Navdeep was with Jagdeep all the time. I called on that number again from which I received the call that day when Jagdeep was attacked. When I inquired about him I came to know that he was my junior who secretly listened to Harpeet's conversation with someone on phone.

I told him to meet me in Celebration mall's parking near C2 pillar at 8PM. I told Navdeep that I would be going to celebration mall just to take a short break and to relax. He was easily convinced by my words and told me to give a call if I needed any help. When I reached there he was already waiting there for me. I recognised him; he was Sukhman famous as Sukh Hacker. He was master of his skills and could hack any account.

I came outside of my car and met him. I asked him to tell me the entire story about what happened that day. He started, "Sir, I was surfing into people's account to see the chats about elections when I saw a weird chat in Harpreet's account. In that chat he sent one photo of Kamal sir to Baljeet's right hand Simar. And the next words in chat were to kill him. After that I tried calling you but your phone was out of network coverage area. I then tried to tap Harpreet's phone calls and finally that evening when he ordered Simar to kill Kamal sir I immediately informed you."

So it was Simar behind this act and was supported by Harpreet and Baljeet. Sukh asked me to take him in our club. I happily agreed to that and told him to accompany me for next one week. I was planning to take revenge from Simar and here the only revenge was to put him to death. Sukh was happy to help at that time because he was not afraid of such things and after that incident with Jagdeep even I was ready to take risk.

From next day, Sukh started taping Simar phone and hacked his facebook account. We were waiting for one moment when he would be alone. Day one we got nothing. He was always with his fellow members. Same thing went for three more days. But finally we got a chance. Simar was very fond of girls; he was having too many girls in his friend list. He was going to meet one of them in Rani Ka Baagh which is famous as lovers point in Amritsar. It was a golden opportunity for us to take him down.

After seeing the conversation, we came to know that they were going to meet at 11PM. They would have been thinking of some private space but they were not aware that for Simar it was going to be his last night. Sukh was not only good at hacking but was also good at managing stuffs. He somehow managed a 9MM Pistol along with 3 bullets in it. In addition to that he was also able to manage silencer to cut off the noise of the fire.

Everything was set, a green bench placed on the corner of the park was the spot where they were going to meet and we were hiding just behind the bench in the bushes which made the boundary of the park. We were expecting Simar to come first but his girl friend was more excited to meet him. She came there 5 minutes earlier and sat down on the bench. As she was waiting for Simar to come we were thinking of how to handle her after shooting Simar.

After few minutes Simar came in his Range rover and met his girl friend. After few minutes of talk they started kissing each other. While sitting there I was thinking that it is going to be his last kiss and on the other side Sukh was enjoying the beauty of the scene. I then decided to let him enjoy his last night with his girl friend and when they will say good bye to each other at that time we will kill him.

After few minutes I went toward his car and started waiting there while Sukh forced me that he will stay there and will text me when Simar will be leaving the place. I waited there for one and half hour. I was looking at Gurleen's photographs with me while I received a message, "He is leaving. Don't leave him this time we will not get such opportunities again and again."

I immediately got behind his car and started watching him while he was approaching towards his car. He went near the door of his range I called out Simar. As he turned back to see me I shot him on his chest. I was shivering in fear and again I took a shot and this time it was on his right shoulder. I cried out loud, "This is for Jagdeep." And finally, when he felt down I took the last shot on this forehead for all the crimes which he had done in his life. He was lying dead in front of me. After few minutes Sukh came near me with his bike and we went away. Mission successful.

HANDLED WITH CARE BY DSP

We straight away went to hospital where Jagdeep was admitted; Kamal and Navdeep were also there. When I told them about what I had done they were like, "This was not expected out of you, and you have this avatar also." I told them how Sukh helped me in killing Simar. Navdeep was little bit worried about the consequences and said, "You know that he was right hand of Baljeet, now it's all about not getting caught. I hope you have not left anything behind."

"Yes don't worry about that Navdeep", I said there.

Police started inquiring about the murder and we were just waiting for the result of that inquiry. There was only one way in which we could have been under suspect i.e. Jagdeep was attacked by him last week. But before anything could happen I got crazy and decided to tell DSP Sidhu everything about what happened that night. I was opposed by everyone when I told this thing in the club. But still I took Sukh along with me to DSP's office.

I told the policeman outside that I wanted to meet DSP. He told me to wait outside and we would be called inside. We sat there for four hours but didn't get a chance to meet him. Next day we again went there and started waiting there. Mean while Sukh said, "Sir maybe because of you he is not willing to talk as such you didn't miss any chance to talk about Gurleen." At that time I wrote something on the visiting card of our club and told the person outside to give it to DSP Sidhu.

Next day, we were first to enter his office. When we were heading toward his cabin, Sukh asked me that what had I written on that card and I replied, "I just wrote that I know who has killed Simar. Please talk to me once." DSP's PA called us inside the office. He reminded me of Gurleen when I saw him sitting in his chair right in front of us. For the time being I got lost in her memories.

DSP began, "So tell me Kanwar, what all you know about the murder of Simar? Or should I tell you what happened that night when you two were there on your bike in rani ka bagh." I got surprised when I heard this. We left no tell traces behind but still he managed to find out something and if so then why were still outside the prison cell. All these things were going around in our minds.

"Kanwar I know that you have killed Simar; what do you think only you can hack others phone calls and messages? Sometimes it's other way round also. These gangster and drug dealers have spoiled half of the Punjab. We were also planning to kill Simar and his subordinates. But when I came to know that one of your friend has been attacked I was sure that you will take some action against it as my daughter told me that you are not afraid of taking risks. So we tapped your phones also."

"Sir then why didn't you arrest us?" I exclaimed.

"Son whatever you have done should have been done by us. You have just helped the police in doing their job. I have heard from Gurleen that you want to become IPS officer and that is the only reason why I took you out of this case. You have not done anything wrong and if you have not done anything wrong then you need not to worry about anything. This seems to be very familiar with you." He smiled and winked at me.

I was about to ask him something related to my love but before I could say anything he stopped me and said, "Now don't ask me anything about my daughter otherwise consequences will not be good. She is happy wherever she is. By the way I just want to say one thing from her side. She doesn't like the profession which you are going to choose. She finds it too risky job for a person like you who is ever ready to do everything for the sake of anything. So think twice before you get into that."

After saying this he asked me that if we would like to have some tea or coffee. I understood that he was trying to say, "Now get the fuck out of my officer." I replied with a no and went outside with his permission. Now the case was solved by the police. We felt quite relaxed at that time but we put our guards down way too early before the final round of the match.

MAIN PLAYER

Baljeet gave me a call on my phone number and told me that he wanted to meet me alone. I was bit scared at that time because going alone was not a good option for me. Someone told me that between brave and dumbass there is only thin line and it is very important that we know the limits of this line. But I still agreed to him and we decided to meet at Crystal restaurant on the Queen's road. Although I informed my friends and DSP Sidhu about this meet but still I was sensing something wrong in that meet. I got a microphone attached to my shirt button to record the whole conversation.

I was waiting for him in the restaurant and it was not surprising for me to see that the whole restaurant was empty. It was pin drop silence in the dining hall and I was wondering that what was going to happen next. When he walked in the through the gate I could see his pistol in the pistol cover hanging by his belt. I tried to show my confidence in front of him that I was not afraid of anything but it was hell lot of a difficult task for me.

He came near me and sat on the seat right in front of me. He took his pistol out and kept it on the centre of the table. It was Glock, automatic pistol. The inner me was saying, "Wow, please give it to me once, I want to try out its firing power." While the outer me said, "Uncle keep it inside, it's the calibre of the machine that matters but the calibre of the man behind the machine. I have done something with an ordinary pistol which anybody else would not even dare to do, even with your pistol."

He smiled and me and said, "Kanwar Singh I have heard a lot about that incident from many places. At first I was surprised that how can someone killed my man that too when I am ruling over the city. But then I was happy because after a long time I have seen someone who can dare to match my standards."

"Not only your standards uncle; I will be over shooting you within a short period of time. Soon we will win the college elections. I don't care who comes in my way I have dedicated my whole and soul for this club and now if anybody dared to stop me will be stopped by aggression of my gun. But don't worry I will not use my gun for you. I will kill you with the same pistol kept on the table right now." I smiled at him after saying that but his face became furious after that.

"I will die according to my own will. There is no one in this world who can kill me. I warn you to get aside of my way and from now onwards I will not warn you again. And about college elections you try your all out to conduct that event first, you will not be able to do that. I promise that our next meeting will not be paid by money but by bloodshed." He said this and walked out of the restaurant.

TRIUMPH WITH LOSS

From next week elections were there and this time we were fully prepared to win. Jagdeep was also discharged from the hospital but he was told to take complete rest in order to make his arm fully functional; so we didn't bothered him much and told him to monitor the internet activities of the college along with Sukh. In college, only we three were the active members at that time.

Finally the day of election, we succeeded in conducting the elections very well and with 80% majority we won the elections. That was the real time to celebrate. Kamal was declared as the president of the Khalsa College. We got best wishes from everywhere but the one which I was waiting for didn't come. I wished that if I could talk to Gurleen but it was not possible. Even though I called DSP Sidhu and told the result but I think that he didn't bother to tell his daughter.

Next weekend we held a party for all the members of the club. That day we decided to tell all the members of the club about the real motive behind all the things which were happening in that house. Kamal took the mike and started, "I would like to thanks all of you present here for having faith in us. First on this youth club and now in the president's elections. We would have not been able to do anything without your support. I want all of you to put your hands together for this friendship, this club and most important for yourself."

Everyone present in the house started clapping and was ready to celebrate victory. But what Kamal said next raised a silent atmosphere in the house. "But, but, but..... There is one thing which is bothering us right now. We have hid something from all of you which I believe that this is the correct time to tell you all."

He took a little bit of pause and then continued, "Friends the real motto of this club is not fitness and not even games. Ladies and gentlemen we are at war with drugs and the drug mafias who are selling these drugs."

There was awkward silence in the house and I wanted Kamal to speak up again otherwise all the people around in no time would start thinking. He continued, "The day we opened this club we knew that something big was going to happen. We had expected the same thing which is happening to us right now. We have been facing end number of warning calls and one of our friends even took bullet for me. But thank god that they have not done anything to any other club member."

"Now what I actually want to say is that till now it was only preparation for war but now the real battle is going to start. I would like to request all of you to please quit this club right other because the way on which we have started walking demands bloodshed and I don't want any one of you to lose your life for no reason. We will take care of it from here onwards. This might be the last time we have gathered here. From now onwards there will be no meeting, no practises for any event however if anyone of you want to continue with gym, he is free to do so but at own risk. And one last thing don't miss the fun tonight enjoy as much as you can."

As he finished his talk, everyone present there stood still in shock. People started talking amongst each other but in low voice. Suddenly the party mood turned into the parting mood. I thought that this might be the last club meeting and after this everything is going to get over. Sukh took the mike from Kamal and started addressing the house.

"I don't know about anyone else present here but I stand with you in this war. All you might be thinking that whatever they are doing is too risky and one or the other day they are going to die but let me tell you one thing what they are doing is not everyone's cup of tea. Not everyone can think of the society around like the way they are thinking. By tomorrow I would like to get the names who all are there along with us and who all want to leave."

Sukh came near us gave all four of us high five. Now we were not four strong but ferocious and fearless five. I asked DJ to play some loud music so that people could enjoy leaving the entire thing which Kamal said few moments before. After that party we five sat together to discuss about the things to be done at that time.

THE PLAN

The only thing which we were waiting for was an opportunity. We were trying to find out Baljeet's weakest link. All we could do at that was hacking. We had done it once in the case Simar and we were pretty much confident that we would get something on which we can work to defeat Baljeet.

One day in the morning Baljeet's PA got a call from an unknown number saying that the delivery of the package would be done on Sunday morning at 4 AM in the morning. We were not aware about what that delivery was all about but in case of Baljeet anyone could guess that it would be related to drugs.

"OK friends, so today is Wednesday and we have got three days to prepare ourselves." Navdeep said in very confident tone.

"What are you planning to do? What should we prepare for?" Kamal asked.

"We will rob that package and will set it on fire. It will be the first official challenge to Baljeet that now there is someone to end his business of drugs and slowly we will end his life." I said with the next level of confidence.

"But how?" Jagdeep asked.

"Find the ways to do so and we will meet tomorrow at same time and same place." I said to end the conversation and we all went to our homes.

As I reached home I called both mom and dad to sit together and told them everything about the club. I also told them what we were going to do with Baljeet. My mother got emotional after listening to that but dad stayed strong. He gave me motivation to continue with the same while mom tried to stop me from doing that. I listened to my dad and told my mom that not to worry about me.

She said me something that pinched my heart.

"Listen son, I just want you to stay out of danger. You are not aware about the after math of these things. I have raised you with lot of expectations you can't do this to me. You always care more about the common people than your loved ones. What if you die, what will I do? For once think about your love

Gurleen what will she do after you are gone?"

I smiled and said, "Mom I forget to tell you that I broke up with Gurleen after that incident I chose my friends and my dreams over her and now she has gone way too far from my life. Don't worry, after this Sunday I am going to leave all this."

After reaching my room I gave a call to DSP Sidhu to inform him everything related to that package. After a long debate he finally agreed to help us on one condition that it was going to be the last activity of this youth club. "After that shut down the club and focus on your careers." I agreed to him as such I was not aiming for anything bigger than that.

Next day we went to the club house to discuss about the plan. DSP Sidhu also came there on my request and now we were all set to take away everything from Baljeet.

"So what is your plan?" DSP Sidhu asked.

"Sir first of all we need to find the route through which the truck will be going and then we will see the most vulnerable point on that road at which we will be able to execute the robbery." Navdeep replied while everyone else was quietly listening.

"Baljeet never go to pick up his package. He just deals with the same only on phone. But he will be present at the place where the truck will be unloading. So it would be better if we catch him red handed and since police is along with us we can finish his chapter then and there only." I said.

"It will be even better if we rob his truck first unloaded it and then take the truck to his place in which all of us will be hiding." Jagdeep said

"Since our motive is to kill him then it will be quite easy for us also. Because there is no point in arresting him and taking to the police station as such he will escape from the same very easily." DSP Sidhu told everyone with a smile on his face.

The plan was set now only execution was left. Sukh was continuously busy with his hacking and stuff while all others were arranging weapons from the same person when had lend us pistol to kill Simar.

On Friday evening we got the route in through which they were travelling and the finish point was at Baljeet's farms on the outer side of his village. We got the number of truck in which the package was coming. We decided to wait for the truck 10 kms away from the village.

EXECUTION

As planned we set the trap for the truck. DSP placed a checking point there about 10 kms away from Baljeet's village at 3AM in the morning. We started following the truck from the mid way of its route and when we came near the check point we overtook it and went ahead of it towards the check point.

Police stopped us there and as told to them we were being checked for the next 20 minutes. In the mean while one policeman went to check the truck. Truck driver just him one thing, "You know it is Baljeet's truck. Don't dare to check it."

Jagdeep also went close to him and told policeman not to check it. Jagdeep also gave him some money so that the checking of the truck could be stopped. Finally policeman as told agreed to him and Jagdeep told the truck driver to take the truck ahead.

Truck driver thanked him and asked his name so that he could tell to his master. Jagdeep in respond asked him to give lift till the farm house. He happily agreed to help Jagdeep.

In the way Jagdeep asked him to stop the truck because he wanted to attend the nature's call. Truck driver asked him to hurry up for he was getting late to deliver the package. From the other side Sukh showed him pistol and told him to surrender the truck to him.

He shouted for Jagdeep's help but he was not aware that Jagdeep was the real culprit. Jagdeep came running and told Sukh not to kill them. He suggested the driver that they should leave the truck and run for their lives. Driver agreed and tried to escape but in few minutes he was caught by DSP Sidhu's team.

Now the new truck driver was Sukh and we four hid ourselves behind the boxes kept in the truck. In next 20 minutes we were in front of Baljeet's farm house.

At the gate, one of his guards stopped the truck and inquired about it. Luckily he was not aware of the driver so we were saved there. He told Sukh to get the truck in the basement. Sukh was first surprised after listening about the basement and then said, "Actually I am new here, can you please show me the way to basement." Guard showed him the way, he followed and texted the same to DSP Sidhu.

Through the garden's backside we entered the basement where Baljeet was waiting for his package. This time Sukh was not only surprised but shocked also after seeing the amount of drugs stored there. Its worth was in billions. Sukh was given his money and was asked to unload the truck there with the help of Baljeet's men. Sukh took four of his men along and started unloading the boxes.

Now it was our time to show up. We were ready with our pistol with silencers attached on them. As they were unloading the boxes each one of us aimed at one of them respectively and took the headshots. All four of them died in no time. But their strength was almost 20 and still 16 of them were left including Baljeet himself.

Sukh called Baljeet saying, "Sir, Can you please help? I am facing problem in unloading the boxes alone."

"I had already given four guys to you how many more you want?" Baljeet inquired.

He sent four more guys and same thing happened with them. Luck didn't favour us at that time when DSP Sidhu entered the scene at wrong time. Suddenly a furious gun fight started there between police and drug mafias.

In the exchange of fire Sukh got hit by bullet in his chest. In few minutes he collapsed down and we were not able to do anything. Baljeet tried to escape from there but we saw him and I went behind him. He was not able to go very far when I fired all my bullets in my pistol on his legs. One bullet luckily got hit and he fell down.

I started hitting him brutally. I was out of my mind as one of my friend died because of him. When he was lying almost dead I asked him, "What did you get after doing all these things?" I was almost crying at that time.

But he smiled and said, "It doesn't matter if I die today or not but you can't stop this sale of drugs in Punjab. There are people who will continue the business. Killing me will not make you win this war, it is a continuous process and you can't do it for your entire life."

I took his pistol from the cover and placed it on his head.

"Shoot me, what are you waiting for. You have lost it my friend, I have lived my life very well but you gave whatever you have in this war. At the end you are left with nothing but disappointments. Because people will not stop using drugs."

Before he could say anything further I shot him with his own pistol.

"As promised as delivered." I said and started crying

When I went back to farm house, the situation was under control. But DSP Sidhu was injured. He got hit by the bullet on the left side of his stomach. He was taken to hospital in the ambulance which was already waiting there outside.

As we reached hospital doctors said, "We have saved him but his condition is very critical right now. Please call someone from his family to take care of him. He needs immense care in this situation. I was not aware where Gurleen was at that point of time but I asked DSP's subordinates to call up his family. He assured me that he will take proper care of him and advised us to leave the city as early as possible.

AFTERMATH

We decided that it would be best for all four of us if we end this club. Final year exams were the only thing left in the college. We all went to different places to save ourselves from any kind of police inquiry or gangster violence.

At that point of time I realised that it is very easy to kill someone but the after math results of the same are much more difficult for a person to handle. Once you get into this then there is no turning back. There is only one dead end to this and that is death. It is said that fortune favours the brave and that is what happened with us.

We escaped that, only because of our luck. Navdeep and Jagdeep started planning for their career in Canada while Kamal got a contract with T-Series for his music career. I also started preparing for IPS and we were all busy thereafter. The only thing which bothered us at that time was Sukh's death.

We decided to talk to his parents and to help them in any way possible. When we talked to them we found that the reason behind Sukh's interest in club was his own brother who was also a victim of drug abuse. He cursed himself daily for he was the reason for his brother's death. But at the end he was able to recover from this drug addiction and finally he was ready to live his life again.

Sumit also escaped the web of drugs and was happily living his life. Later on I found that by losing one life we were able to give hundreds of people a new life in which they were ready to start from a new beginning. Even after losing everything because of drugs they were ready to start from zero and that too with great enthusiasm.

That was the success of our club. On one side all these people were ready to support us in this war against drugs and one side it was the promise which I made to my mom and DSP Sidhu. I am a man of my words so in spite of my will to do something I quit.

That day was the worst day of my life. I was standing nowhere. Neither my love was with me nor was I able to fulfil my dreams. Once in a lifetime you fall in love and same goes for war be it against anything, but at that of time I failed in both. I gave up so early in both just because I was selfish.

Not everyone can be Bhagat Singh, not everyone can think of sacrificing life for the nation, it requires guts. It is said that no guts no glory, no sacrifice no story. I could not afford any other life of my loved ones to be sacrificed. Baljeet rightly said that it is a continuous process. We couldn't think of fighting against it for long time. Even if we could we refused to do so.

No more college after that. We only went for our final exams. We used to meet after exams but now it was not like earlier. Now I was afraid of losing my friends also but thank God the everlasting bond of friendship proved itself. After final exams we all parted from each other but we promised to be in touch with each other.

Navdeep and Jagdeep went to Canada and Kamal went to Australia for his music album. Now it was only me, left alone along with the memories of college life and of course of my love. Although I cleared the IPS exam after one year but I didn't join. I had some personal reasons for that which was again criticised by the people around.

EPILOUGE

After a long talk I told everyone to visit my house and to meet my son. Everyone was surprised when I said that, "When did you got married, you bastard you didn't even thought of inviting us huh?" Navdeep complained.

"Yaar it happened 3 years ago. I wanted to keep it as a surprise for all of you so that when we meet I would have something new to tell. But I bet that you will like my better half in the first meet itself."

We all started moving toward my house, everyone was giving me an intense look. I was just smiling at that time and finally when we reached home I took them to the guest room and called my son. His mother was carrying him along.

All three of them said in a combined tune, "Gurleen."

Navdeep said, "You are such an idiot. If you were going to marry her then what was the problem in telling us?"

All of them just jumped over me and started beating me just for fun and because they were angry at me. Gurleen tried to stop them and finally she requested me to tell them the whole story.

And then I begun,

When I cleared my IPS entrance exam I went to Gurleen's dad to tell him the good news. I thought that he might be very happy for I promised him to be successful in my life. But when I went there and told him everything he was very sad.

He said, "Son I told you that my daughter didn't want you to become IPS officer but you still chose this profession."

Before I could say anything in my defence I saw Gurleen entering his room. We both saw each other and in next few moments we started crying. She came towards me and hugged me tightly.

DSP Sidhu told me that he wanted her daughter to marry me for I was a changed person by then. Also that her fiancé left just because of one reason that she was not able to get rid of me and my memories of love. I didn't tell you this before because I didn't want you to shift your focus away from your goal. But the only thing he was afraid of was my job and that too because of my attitude.

I talked to Gurleen and it was like a thirsty man roaming around in desert for water suddenly found a pound of the same. She just asked me one thing that I should quit my dream of IPS officer and should do something else.

I had lost her once in my life and was not ready to commit the same mistake. She was ready to be mine and was desperate to get her back in my life. So I decided to let go the IPS job.

I called my mom and told her everything. She was very happy after hearing that and said, "Son you will get end number of job opportunities in your life but you will not get another chance to marry her. Go on, I am with you."

Sometime you have to give up on your dreams for your loved ones, sometime you have to take risk in life in order to be successful and sometime you have to lose one thing over other but believe me if your one decision can make your loved ones stay in your life then you should positively take that decision even if it demands a sacrifice from your side.

After one year we got married and it was not like all other Punjabi weddings where people spend lakhs of rupees on celebration. It was quite simple one and I didn't want to bother you all for coming as such it was just the beginning of your careers.

And now the fact is that we all are well settled in our lives. Thank you everyone for being in my life. Thank you so much to each and everyone present here, it's only because of you that today I have got such memories in my life which can make me laugh and cry at any point of time. It all depends which part of it you want to recall and relive.

At last- All is well when the end is well.

www.ingramcontent.com/pod-product-compliance
Lightning Source LLC
Chambersburg PA
CBHW050131170726

47995CB00001BA/344